EXT MONSTERS™

WHAT'S WITH WULF?

BY LOUISE SIMONSON
ILLUSTRATED BY JAMES W. ELSTON

Extreme Monsters™ created
by Randy Meredith and Eric Smith

A Penny Candy Press™ Book

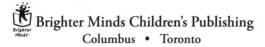
Brighter Minds Children's Publishing
Columbus • Toronto

Cover Illustration by Eric Smith

Library of Congress Control Number: 2005931100

ISBN 1-57791-179-2

www.pennycandypress.com

Printed in the United States of America

1   2   3   4   5   09   08   07   06   05

I dedicate this book with admiration to Nikolai Muth, Siddhartha Heyes, Adelaine Muth, and Sylvanna Gross who work extremely hard at school and sports with excellent results.

Many thanks to Thomas Kintner, Extreme Sports Advisor extraordinaire for his advice on verts, half pipes, spins, grinds, grabs and slides

CONTENTS

CHAPTER ONE

The Big Blow-Up

"Anybody got the ultimate spectacular stunt worked up for the charity event?" Wulf asked.

Fur flying, the young werewolf zipped backwards on his in-line skates, circling the interior of the garage where the Extreme Monsters Extreme Sports Team held their regular meetings. He stared at each face as he went by and was greeted with a blank stare in return.

"No? Dudes! We only have three more days! Saving the Croney Island roller coaster is the most important thing we'll do this year!"

Mumford, a smallish boy wrapped mummy-like from head to toe in bandages, was pointing his brand-new video camera at Wulf, trying to record the young werewolf's dramatic leaps over extreme sports equipment and teammates that found themselves in his path.

But Mumford was having problems. Maybe the wrappings on his fingers made it hard to hit the right button. Could the glue from his bandages be mucking up the moving parts? Something was wrong because the warning light kept blinking on. Mumford tried using the tentacle-like ends of his wrappings to hold the camera steady, but he couldn't keep the speedy Wulf in focus.

Showing off for the camera, Wulf pivoted and did a 360 spin over the head of Steiner. The rather large boy with greenish skin glanced up at Wulf. He scratched his squarish head. Steiner looked back down at the freewheel of his BMX motocross bike, absent-mindedly touched the bolt in his neck and then went back to fiddling with the bike's sprocket.

Wulf darted around Val, the young half vampire who led the team. Val kept spinning on his skateboard to keep Wulf in view.

Wulf did a back flip over the young witch, Jinx, the team's only girl. Jinx was sitting cross-legged on her street luge, her nose buried in her spell book. She was muttering incantations and making little dips and waves with her wand, completely ignoring Wulf's antics. Bela, her pet bat and the team mascot, was perched on the point of her hat. Bela ducked worriedly as the young werewolf flew overhead.

As Mumford tried to track Wulf's movements, the camera's warning light came on again. Mumford banged the case in frustration. *Who am I kidding?* he thought miserably. *I'm no sports photographer.*

Heck, he wasn't even sure the camera was turned on. Mumford thought that he should have read the instructions. Maybe Wulf was wrong when he told Mumford that "Reading instructions is for wimps."

Mumford sighed. He was always scared he'd do the wrong thing and blow it. Sometimes being the youngest Extreme Monster stunk!

"What trick are you going to do for the benefit, Wulf?" Val asked. "I know that old roller coaster used to be your favorite ride. You were mad when they shut it down."

Mumford focused the camera on Val. Val was spinning gracefully on his skateboard, easily following Wulf's dramatic circling, but he wasn't showing off to get attention. Val didn't have to. There was something about the young vampire that drew every eye. *Star Quality*, Mumford thought. That's what the TV special on skateboarding said Val had.

Mumford swung the camera back to the zooming Wulf.

"I haven't decided what stunt to do," Wulf said. "But it will be even more spectacular than that frontside tailslide kickflip grind you demoed on that TV special. Something even more amazing. Death defying, even!"

It was Mumford's theory that Wulf wanted to prove he had star quality, too. That's why he wanted to be filmed. Mumford guessed Wulf was a bit jealous of Val.

9

"Shutting down the roller coaster was bad enough, dudes!" Wulf cried dramatically "Now, the stupid park owners are talking about tearing it down. If we don't raise enough money to restore it, those jerks will bring in the wrecking ball!"

"They're not jerks!" said Jinx, looking up from her spell book. "And they're talking about tearing the roller coaster down before it falls down and kills someone. That's what's called a responsible attitude!"

"Responsible? Ha!" Wulf growled, skidding to a stop right in front of her. "Trashing that ride would be criminal! It's practically a historic landmark!"

Mumford swiveled his camera from Wulf to Jinx, then back to Wulf. Now that Wulf was holding still, maybe he could get a decent shot. But as Mumford peered through the lens, the image blurred again.

"Stupid auto focus!" Mumford muttered, slamming the camera with his bandaged fist. The thing was going to drive him crazy.

Beyond the camera, Jinx's red eyes were flashing angrily at Wulf. "The park owners are concerned about public safety! They're trying to do the right thing!"

The hair along Wulf's neck bristled. In a low voice he snarled, "You're out of your mind!"

Jinx leapt to her feet. "Well, you wouldn't recognize responsibility if it bit you on the tail!"

"Time out, guys!" Val said, making a "T" with his

hands. He flew up into the air. Val was tired of spinning on his board to follow Wulf's movements and knew his flight would draw their attention. Being half vampire had its advantages.

Hovering among the rafters, Val frowned down at Wulf and Jinx. "Jinx, are you saying you don't want to be part of the benefit exhibition to save the roller coaster?" he asked.

"Of course not!" Jinx huffed, staring at her teammates in exasperation. "What I'm saying is that all of your monster powers come naturally—like Val having super-hearing and being able to fly and turn into mist. Or Steiner's strength and his ability to heal. Or Wulf's strength and agility. Even Mumford can move his bandages like tentacles. But I have to learn witchcraft! I have to do that wimpy thing," she said, glaring at Wulf.

Wulf frowned suspiciously. "What wimpy thing?"

Jinx waved her book and wand under his nose. "The thing I heard you tell Mumford was dumb. You know—reading the *instructions? Memorizing* them? *Following* them? I have to study spells and learn to use magic properly, or someone could get hurt! Acing my seventh level Spelling Bee is just as important to me as working up a trick to help save some crumbling—"

Wulf growled angrily. "It *will* crumble, unless we save it! Look, if nobody but me is interested in saving the roller coaster, maybe I should do the benefit alone!"

From his place among the rafters, Val signaled to Mumford to put down the camera. Val hoped that if no one was recording the argument, Wulf and Jinx would settle down.

Mumford tossed the camera onto a workbench, hoping maybe it would break. He didn't care if he ever picked it up again.

"Wulf! Stop it!" Val ordered. "You're way out of line! Jinx isn't your enemy! And Jinx—"

Steiner looked up from fixing the sprocket of his BMX bike. "We hear you, Jinx," he said calmly, "but Croney Island wouldn't be the same without that old roller coaster." He wiggled his eyebrows comically, causing his stitched forehead to crinkle like cellophane.

Jinx glanced over at Steiner. He looked big and hard, but his heart was warm and soft. He hated to see his teammates argue. Wiggling his eyebrows, he looked so silly Jinx couldn't help smiling.

"I guess—" she began.

"I'm right! Admit it!" Wulf chortled triumphantly. "So put your stupid book away, Jinx, and let's concentrate on what's important. This is team time. You can study later!"

With a lightning-fast move, Wulf snatched the spell book and wand from Jinx's hands and skated off.

Bela the bat flapped into the air. "Trouble!" he squeaked. "Better hide!"

"Give those back, Wulf! Didn't you listen to anything I said?" Jinx yelled, starting after him.

"Sure, I did," said Wulf, skating backwards and waving the opened book over his head. "You said learning spells is hard. But I think you're making a big deal out of nothing. I think anyone can do it!"

Peering into the opened spell book, Wulf began to read some phrases. Soon he switched to making them up, whenever he thought of lines that rhymed. He was waving the wand like a conductor's baton, enjoying his fun at Jinx's expense.

"Ice cream, popcorn, lemon twist..." Wulf spun the book out of Jinx's reach just in time. "Dudette, I thought you were studying magic, not cooking!" He jerked the book left, causing Jinx to fall on top of Mumford.

"Don't!" Jinx yelled, dashing after him. "I wasn't kidding, Wulf. One wrong word or dip of the wand could cause a disaster!"

Jinx sidestepped over one of Steiner's spare pedals and looked up again. Wulf had said something else. Suddenly, a soft humming noise surrounded them.

Oh no! thought Jinx. *Please don't let this be happening.* Jinx dove for the book but missed. She landed hard on the floor. Rubbing her sore neck, she saw that Wulf was still waving the wand.

The noise got louder. Jinx called up to the hovering Val. "This isn't a joke! We have to stop him!"

Val didn't know precisely why Jinx sounded so worried. He heard the sound, but didn't know what it meant. He did know Wulf's teasing had gone on long enough. Val flew toward the circling werewolf.

"Game's over, Wulf!" he said sternly, as he plucked the spell book from Wulf's hand. "Now cut it out!"

But Wulf still had the wand. Waving it fancifully, he skated backwards, away from Jinx and Val. He was in a groove now, so gleefully determined to extend his fake spell joke, that he didn't even notice when the garage began to shake.

Steiner looked around. "What's going on?"

"Earthquake?" asked Mumford nervously.

"It's Wild Magic!" Jinx cried. "Wulf's spell just released it! Duck, everybody! Now!"

Jinx, Steiner, and Mumford threw themselves on the floor. Val flattened himself against the ceiling. The flapping Bela buried himself in Val's hair.

The humming became a strong rumble. Soon it echoed as loud as thunder. A beam of light leapt from the wand and ricocheted around the garage. Then— bang! It struck Wulf full in the forehead.

Blinding energy filled the garage. Workbenches flew into the air and slammed against the walls. Knocked out by the blast of energy, the Extreme Monsters collapsed into unconsciousness.

PUZZLE 1

Directions:

Solve the crossword puzzle, then follow the directions below to discover the first number of your secret code.

ACROSS
4. The Spelling Bee level Jinx was studying to take
5. The youngest Extreme Monster
6. Jinx has _____ eyes

DOWN
1. Wulf snatched the _____ and wand from Jinx
2. Val has _____ quality
3. Mumford has a new video _____
4. Steiner was fixing a _____ on his bike.

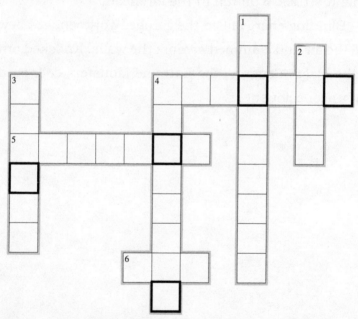

After you've solved the crossword, write the five letters in the boxed squares down on a piece of paper. Unscramble the letters to form a word for a number between one and ten.

Write the number in the CODE KEY on page 93.

CHAPTER TWO

Where's Wulf?

Jinx groaned and opened her eyes. She was lying on her back staring up at the garage ceiling. Val was draped over one of the rafters with Bela tangled in his hair.

Val opened his eyes. "What happened?" he asked in a shaky voice.

"Good question!" Jinx muttered.

She sat up and looked around. The place was a mess. Workbenches were up-ended. Equipment lay in pieces on the floor. Tools poked out of the walls at odd angles. Trophies were scattered all over.

Steiner and Mumford were lying nearby, out cold. As Jinx watched, Steiner groaned and Mumford opened his eyes.

At least we're alive, thought Jinx. She started to piece together what happened. She remembered that Wulf had the spell book and wand, that he was pretending to do magic and then there was a flash of light.

Jinx looked around frantically. Her book and wand lay abandoned in opposite corners of the garage.

But Wulf wasn't there. Wulf was gone.

The side door to the garage was opened just a crack. "Wulf must have gone outside!" said Mumford.

Which means he hasn't magicked himself out of existence, Jinx thought, with a sigh of relief.

The four friends went out to take a look. No Wulf. Val and Steiner checked inside Val's house, while Jinx and Mumford went next door to check Jinx's house. Wulf wasn't there.

They asked Jinx's neighbor, Mrs. Watson, who was outdoors planting flowers in her garden, if she'd seen Wulf go by. She thought she remembered seeing him go that way, she told them, pointing toward Wulf's house down the street. Together, they trotted to Wulf's house. No one was home.

"We can't have been unconscious long," Val told his team as they trudged back to Val's garage. "He can't have gotten far."

But Jinx knew that Wulf could skate like lightning. If he wanted to, he could be so far away they'd never find him. She paced around the garage as Steiner reassembled his bike.

"But why would he leave?" Mumford asked. "Does he think we're mad at him?"

"Nah!" said Steiner. "He's lost his temper and done crazy things plenty of times. We'll forgive him, like we always do."

"It would be more like *him* to be mad at *us*," muttered Jinx. "At me!" She bit her lip. "I called him irresponsible and dissed the roller coaster he's so wild to save."

"And I grabbed your book away from him and told him he was out of line. He's probably mad at me, too," Val agreed.

"I'll bet he's at Croney Island right now, working on his stunt for the benefit. And working off his mad," said Jinx, starting to feel cheerful for the first time all afternoon.

She ignored the little voice that suggested Wulf must have been somehow changed by the Wild Magic that struck him. That he would never have abandoned unconscious teammates if he'd been in his right mind. Leaping to her feet, Jinx said, "I'll run next door and grab my skates. We'll go find him!"

Jinx sped across town on her in-line skates. Skating wasn't her favorite sport. She preferred the rush of the sled-like street luge. The problem was that the luge only ran downhill, and you definitely couldn't take it on city streets.

Val skateboarded beside her. Mumford was skitching a ride with Steiner, two feet were placed squarely on his board and one bandage attached to the back of the BMX bike.

The Extreme Monsters sped toward the entrance to the Croney Island Amusement Park, flashed their passes at the human guard who grinned and waved them through, then wheeled straight for the rickety old coaster and the nearby demo area.

Wulf wasn't there either.

"What now?" Jinx asked.

Feeling more and more anxious, they searched the Monsterey Valley Extreme Sports Park. No Wulf. They peered in the window of Mr. Cool's Ice Cream and Beet Juice Parlor. No Wulf. They whizzed past the Pendant Towers building, owned by their archenemy Damon Christopher, who also owned the extreme sports group known as Team Pendant.

"Wulf couldn't be in there, could he?" asked Jinx, pointing worriedly at the soaring structure.

Steiner snorted. "Wulf knows the score. He'd never go near that place."

Steiner would know. He'd been Team Pendant's BMX motocross ace—actually more like its prisoner— until Val made a bet with Damon Christopher that freed Steiner from his Pendant contract.

Jinx shrugged. As far as the Extreme Monsters were concerned, Team Pendant only existed to advertise Damon Christopher's shoddy sports products. The team had talent, but most of the extreme athletes on the circuit knew that Damon insisted that his team cheat at every opportunity to ensure a win. Only airtight contracts and barely-veiled threats had kept Damon's secret from the adoring public, who rushed to buy Pendant gear at every opportunity.

Jinx looked over at Val. "Now what?"

The Monsters checked the schoolyard, the arcade, the movie theater, the mall, even the polluted swamp on the other side of town where Christopher's main henchmen, the Slime Brothers, liked to hang out. Wulf was nowhere to be found.

Worried and dejected, the four Extreme Monsters trudged past Mr. Cool's on the way back to Val's garage.

"I'm hot!" said Mumford, looking wistfully toward the air-conditioned interior.

"And thirsty!" added Steiner.

"Come on, gang! Let's get something cold," Val said. "We can worry here just as well as in the garage."

Mumford snapped several bandages around Steiner's bike so that it was solidly chained to the curbside rack. The group went inside.

At the counter, Mr. Cool, an abominable snowman with white hair in a short summer buzz-cut, served cones to Jinx, Mumford, and Steiner. Val, the health-conscious vegetarian, asked for a sparkling beet juice.

"Over there!" said Jinx, leading the way to an empty table.

Licking her double scoop of Magic-Mallow, Jinx flopped into a seat and sighed mightily. She leaned her head back, soothing her still-injured neck muscles. She gazed at a really cool pair of roller-blades hanging from a peg high on the wall. She stared at the skates and thought it was odd that they had the Extreme Monster logo on them. Jinx nearly dropped her cone.

"Aren't those Wulf's?" cried Jinx.

Steiner, the tallest Monster, lifted the skates down. "These are Wulf's, all right," he said grimly.

"He must be really mad at us if he left his team skates here," Val said, sounding worried.

"Does this mean Wulf's given up on the Extreme Monsters?" Mumford asked anxiously. "Doesn't he want to be part of our team anymore?"

"I don't know what it means," Val said solemnly.

Steiner sighed. "I guess we better tell Doc."

Doc, the team's coach and brilliant all-around technical wizard, scratched his head as the monsters finished telling him the whole sad story.

"I don't see a problem," he said. "Lycanthropes—of which werewolves are a species—are night creatures. Once the moon comes out, Wulf will settle down. He'll turn up tomorrow at Croney Island, operating at full

capacity and eager for our practice and photo session. You'll see. Wulf would do anything to save that roller coaster," Doc chuckled. "Even forgive the four of you!"

Jinx sighed. The gangly man with silver hair and a bristling moustache was the smartest man she knew. He had invented many of the devices used in extreme sporting, including Neutralizer Wristbands that repressed the monsters' special powers, so that humans and monsters could compete together as equals. He was a technical genius in every respect. But as a man of science, he was less knowledgeable in the ways of magic and often underestimated how tricky they could be. Except for his skates, there was no sign of Wulf. And this told Jinx there was every reason to worry.

The next morning, Doc drove his Laboratory Utility Vehicle through the entrance to the Croney Island Amusement Park and onto the demo lot set up beside the roller coaster. Steiner, who had no parents and lived with Doc, jumped down from the passenger seat and greeted Val, Jinx, and Mumford.

"Wulf's not here?" Steiner asked, as he off-loaded his bike from the back of the van.

Val looked around. "Not yet," he said.

Doc swung down from the driver's seat. "Wulf won't miss practice. He'll come!"

Doc smiled. More photographers and reporters than he had expected were converging on the Extreme Monsters, eager for interviews and pictures to promote the upcoming benefit.

"Why don't you four work on your routines while these nice folks take your pictures?" said Doc, shooing the kids toward the stunt demo area.

At that moment, a cyclops reporter for *The Monster Times* shouted out, "Where's Wulf?"

Jinx's skin turned a little greener than usual. She shook her head and looked around "I don't feel so good," she mumbled. "I think I'll sit this photo-op out." Jinx walked over and took a seat on a bench.

The other Monsters went through their routines without much spirit. Val showcased part of his skateboard demo. Steiner did the requisite hot-dogging on his BMX. Mumford demonstrated his big-wall style speed climbing. And Jinx sat in the stands, playing with her wand.

The photographers took a lot of pictures. The reporters asked a lot of questions...about Wulf, mostly. Which made Jinx's stomach hurt even more. She wondered if the reporters knew a secret the Extreme Monsters didn't.

Jinx's head swiveled constantly, searching for Wulf, so she was the first to notice the stretch Hummer pull onto the demo lot. "Who's that?" Jinx called out to the others.

Val, Mumford, and Steiner quit their routines to turn and stare at the Hummer. As it slowed to a stop, they saw the Team Pendant logo on its side. "This is our photo-op!" Val muttered angrily. "What's Team Pendant doing here?"

The passenger door of the Hummer opened. As the Extreme Monsters gaped, out stepped Wulf. His normally floppy hair was slicked back and partially covered by a gold beret. His sunglasses were studded with jewels, and a pearl earring dangled from one ear. The macho bling-bling dangling from his neck set off his gold lamé vest.

The reporters made a beeline for the Hummer. Snap! Whirrr! went the cameras as Wulf struck pose after pose beside the Team Pendant logo—the very image of cool.

"Doc told us Wulf would show!" Steiner muttered to Val.

"That *can't* be Wulf!" Val whispered back.

"What's wrong with Wulf?" wailed Mumford.

But Jinx knew. Her heart sank as she saw how the magic had transformed him...and not for the better.

Wulf moved aside and Team Pendant owner Damon Christopher stepped regally down to join him. Damon straightened his silk tie, then put a manicured hand on Wulf's shoulder. He cleared his throat and held up a hand to quiet the reporters.

"I you all will excuse me, I have an announcement to make," he said. "Wulf has left the Extreme Monsters. From now on, he will compete as Team Pendant's superstar blader!"

PUZZLE 2

Directions:

Below is a list of some of the places the other Extreme Monsters looked for Wulf, but not in the right order. Write a "1" on the blank next to the first place they looked for Wulf, write a "2" on the blank next to the second place they looked for Wulf and continue until you have all the locations marked with numbers in the exact order they visited each location.

_____ Croney Island Amusement Park

_____ Val's House

_____ Polluted Swamp

_____ Pendant Towers

_____ Wulf's House

_____ Extreme Sports Park

_____ Mr. Cool's Ice Cream & Beet Juice Parlor

_____ Jinx's House

Write the Polluted Swamp's number in the secret code box provided on page 93.

CHAPTER THREE

A Swell Contract

Val looked at Jinx. Jinx looked at Val. Their mouths were hanging open. Wulf has joined Team Pendant?

Doc was almost as stunned as they were. "Tell me this isn't happening!" moaned Steiner. Mumford was trying not to cry.

"It's the spell Wulf did!" said Jinx. "It was Wild Magic! It warped his mind!"

"No kidding!" said Val. "Let's try to talk to him."

Val led the others toward the shouting mass of reporters and photographers who formed a human wall around Wulf and Damon. "This is what those reporters were waiting for," Jinx said angrily. "Damon must have leaked the scoop about Wulf switching teams. That's why the reporters kept asking us about him."

Val nodded as he craned his neck to get a better look at Wulf. Only Steiner, who was taller than everyone else, could see him.

"Why did you leave the Extreme Monsters?" shouted a reporter in the front.

The team members couldn't believe their ears. They actually heard Wulf's voice say, "Extreme Monsters? What are you talking about? Everyone knows I am *The* Extreme Monster!"

Jinx rolled her eyes. "*The* Extreme Monster? Puh-lease!"

As the four friends made their way to the back of the crowd, reporters shouted more questions.

"I want you all to know that Wulf here came to me on his own," answered Damon Christopher. "I did no coercing or cajoling. Wulf just knew that Team Pendant is the only team that can offer all the best to a skater of his caliber. And as The Extreme Monster, he will be the centerpiece of our team! He will be the Team Pendant superstar!"

"Oh, man," Steiner groaned. "I hope Wulf didn't sign a contract with that lying jerk! If Val hadn't rescued me, I'd still be Damon's slave!"

"A contract!" Jinx gasped, horrified. "He couldn't! He wouldn't! Steiner, pretend you're a reporter!"

"What?!" said Steiner. "Why?"

"I don't have time to explain!" Jinx whispered. "Just ask Wulf if he's signed a contract! Do it!"

Jinx snapped her fingers and her wand appeared in her hand. She began pushing her way into the crowd of reporters. As she worked her way toward Wulf, she considered spell after spell. There had to be one that would work. Then she had it. Jinx knew exactly what to do. If only—

Another babble of shouted questions peppered the air. Steiner's bellow was the loudest of them all: "Wulf, have you signed a contract yet?" Wulf didn't answer. It was as if he couldn't hear Steiner talking.

Several other reporters shouted out the same question: "Have you signed a contract?"

"Not yet, dudes! But I am pumped to be with the best!" Wulf answered.

"His signing ceremony will take place this evening, carried live, exclusively, on Pendant Enterprises' own Satellite Extreme Sports Channel," said Damon smoothly. "You are all invited to the ceremony, the most important event in extreme team sports this year!"

Not if I can stop it! Jinx thought fiercely.

There were more shouted questions, but the billionaire owner said, "Thank you, gentlemen, ladies. That will be all for now!"

Jinx had nearly reached the front of the crowd when she heard the door of the Hummer opening. She was going to be too late! Already muttering her spell, Jinx burst through the final ring of reporters and found herself face-to-face with Wulf.

Jinx stared into Wulf's eyes, but Wulf looked right

through her. Damon Christopher had Wulf by the arm. He was half inside the Hummer, trying to tug Wulf in with him, but Wulf was busy smiling and posing.

Wulf raised his right fist. "Save the Croney Island roller coaster!" he shouted. "That's what it's all about!" He looked right at Jinx and his expression didn't change. He still didn't see her. She didn't exist.

Jinx told herself not to let it bother her, since she had no idea what the magic had done to him. She finished her spell:

Read the contract's small print well.
Skip this step, your hand will swell!

Jinx flicked her wand. The magic landed right where she had aimed it.

"Ow!" said Wulf, grabbing his raised fist.

"What happened?" Damon asked him.

"I don't know," Wulf said, rubbing his hand. "I think something stung me!"

"No problem," said Damon, practically shoving Wulf into the Hummer. "You don't skate with your hands!"

The door slammed shut and the Hummer drove away. The crowd of reporters turned on Val, Jinx, Steiner, and Mumford, shoving microphones in their faces and shouting, "How do you feel about your ex-teammate joining your greatest rivals?"

*****

"How did they think we would feel?" Val muttered angrily, as he watched the reporters dash off to report their stories.

Jinx sighed. "Maybe we should have told them the truth about Wulf hexing himself."

"We couldn't," said Steiner. "It would sound like sour grapes. Besides, who'd believe Wulf would do a dumb thing like that?"

"Somebody who knew Wulf?" Mumford said. The Extreme Monsters couldn't help smiling. Of all the impulsive stunts Wulf had pulled, this was easily the worst.

Jinx's smile faded. "I was standing in front of Wulf and he looked right through me."

"He must have heard my voice, but he didn't answer me, either," Steiner said slowly.

"He's ignoring us—pretending we don't exist!" grumbled Mumford.

"We're just Extreme Monsters. He's *The* Extreme Monster!" Val said bitterly.

"It's annoying," said Jinx. "But maybe he can't help it. He *is* under a spell! And it's not all his fault. I mean... he was being annoying and showing off, but I didn't have to lose my temper and yell at him." Jinx hung her head. "It was my fault, too."

"And mine," Val sighed. "I knew he was feeling a little jealous of the TV show. I didn't have to be so bossy."

"Hey, man, I just ignored him. That's even worse!" said Steiner.

"How can we save him?" asked Mumford.

Jinx put her arm around the small boy's shoulder. "We'll give it our best shot, Mumfy. But it may take a while to undo the spell. If it's even possible. Can anyone remember exactly what Wulf said and did?"

"Some of it," said Steiner.

"A little. I think," mumbled Mumford .

Val sighed. "Not much. And we have a more immediate problem. Damon said Wulf is going to sign his Pendant contract tonight."

Jinx laughed. "Oh, I don't think we need to worry about that!"

"Why?" Val asked suspiciously. He turned to stare at the young witch. "Jinx, what did you do?"

"Let's watch the show tonight," she said. "Let's just see what happens!"

That evening, the four Monsters sat around the television in Val's den, eating popcorn. Val sipped his sparkling beet juice while the rest of the gang drank soda. The logo for Damon's Satellite Extreme Sports Channel flashed on the screen. The television showed a fancy room lined with trophies. Giant pictures of Wulf in Pendant gear were positioned next to several pictures of a smiling Damon Christopher. An announcer was saying in a hushed voice, "This is where the most important signing in extreme sports history will take place. A signing so significant that the officials here at the Satellite Extreme Sports Channel have decided to cancel all regular programming to bring you this amazing event live."

A handful of popcorn bounced off the screen. "The officials? PLEASE!" yelled Jinx impatiently. "The station is owned by Damon Christopher. Of course they would cancel a rerun of Pendant Sports Profile for this!"

The television showed a high table with the contract prominently displayed on it. Beside the contract perched the Team Pendant mascot, Vincent the raven. A loud brass fanfare faded into a driving beat. Spotlights swirled and whirled. Strobe lights flashed. And then it all stopped.

The spotlights zeroed in on a single spot on the floor. The floor opened, and Wulf and Damon Christopher rose slowly up as fireworks flashed around them. The young werewolf was covered with gold chains.

"Nice and understated," said Val.

The five members of Team Pendant stepped in behind them. Among them were Chip Brentwood and Scott Squire, two extreme athletes who were good enough they didn't need Christopher's cheating ways. There was a new girl that Val didn't recognize. That wasn't surprising, as Damon seemed to hire and fire team members on a whim. Two were monsters—tall, green, warty, super-strong teenagers with green skin and long, greasy, green hair. They were known as the Slime Brothers, for their ability to ooze toxic gunk from the palms of their hands.

Jinx ate a fistful of popcorn. "The Slime Brothers are nearly as ugly on TV as they are in real life."

Steiner snorted. "Up till now, they've been Damon's favorite henchmen."

"They're looking at Wulf like they want to flatten him," said Mumford, sounding worried.

"You're right," Val said seriously. "Those goons must feel threatened. They'll try to hurt Wulf if they can."

On the television, Damon and Wulf stood beside the table. The contract was in front of them. Damon took a gold pen from a red velvet pillow and offered it to Wulf so he could sign on the dotted line.

"Don't do it, man!" Steiner covered his face. "Tell me when its over!"

"It'll be okay." Jinx said. "I hope!" She crossed her fingers.

The television showed a close-up of Wulf's hand taking the pen. As the friends watched, Wulf's hand began to swell, as if someone was blowing it up like a balloon. The fingers grew fatter and fatter, until it looked like they were about to explode.

The camera cut to Damon Christopher, who was watching in horror. Vincent the raven squawked twice and flew off. The pen fell from Wulf's bulbous fingers and bounced onto the floor. Wulf shrugged.

"Dude! What's the deal?" he said, looking at his hand in confusion. Damon looked at the growing hand with suspicion. He glanced around as if suspecting foul play. Wulf slapped a fly on the side of his head with the big hand, and nearly knocked himself over.

"Ooooh!" Wulf said. "This must be a reaction to the bug bite I got at the press conference earlier. I guess I'm allergic?" Wulf looked right at the camera and held up his swollen hand. "Doesn't matter! I can still skate! What matters is saving the Croney Island roller coaster because I am the best, the all-time greatest, *The* Extreme Monster!"

"Wow!" murmured Steiner. "With everything that's happened, Wulf's still going on about that ride!"

"Shhhh!" said the others.

"And Wulf will be at the Croney Island Roller Coaster Benefit," Damon interrupted, "bringing glory to Team Pendant!" Damon lifted Wulf's swollen hand high and glared straight at the audience. "This...allergic reaction..." Damon paused as he stared at the hand suspiciously. "...Will merely postpone the signing. I

guarantee that I, Damon Christopher, am bringing Wulf to the greatest action sports company on the planet. You can bank on it!"

The screen showed the Satellite Extreme Sports Channel logo, then switched to a commercial.

"I wouldn't count that money right away," Val said to the television. He turned to his friends. "Looks like Wulf's head isn't the only thing that's swollen."

The Monsters burst out laughing.

They looked over at Jinx who was dancing around the room, pumping her fist into the air, shouting, "I knew he wouldn't read the fine print! Three cheers for wimps who like to read and practice their spelling homework!"

PUZZLE 3

Directions:

Uh-oh! The words for Jinx's spell got scrambled! Put them in the right order on the blanks below!

small	step	the	hand	your	contract's	
well	read	print	swell	this	will	skip

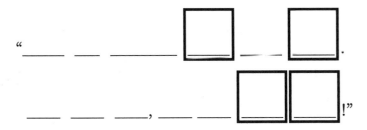

Four of the words above have a square around them. Write the letter that all four of those words have in common in the secret code box provided on page 93.

CHAPTER FOUR

Saving the Superstar

"Another photo-op?" Wulf asked the next morning, as he bladed beside Damon Christopher on the way to the Team Pendant practice track. *"The* Extreme Monster doesn't need more press. I'm already the number one attraction, Dude. What I need is to practice. And I need to come up with an awesomely spectacular stunt—"

"Yes!" Damon interrupted enthusiastically. "The stunt that will put Team Pendant's name—and, uh, your name, of course—in lights! That will have Team Pendant at the top of every extreme sports list! That will have people rushing to the stores—"

"—a stunt that will showcase my star quality," Wulf continued, "and inspire generous donations to save the Croney Island roller coaster!"

"The most important thing about today's photo-op is you'll be wearing the official Team Pendant uniform and the official Team Pendant skates," said Damon, ignoring Wulf's blather. "Reporters and cameramen from all the major news organizations will be here soon!"

Val hovered over Wulf and Damon Christopher. He loved having the ability to turn to mist and float around unnoticed. Today Val's mist looked like just another wisp of Monsterey smog, as he crept over the surrounding wall and into Team Pendant's practice yard.

The place was amazing, heavily equipped for both street and vert-style action. It featured a racetrack with ramps of varying heights, three, six, and twelve foot half pipes, plus an eleven-foot vert, and a number of high and low rails and bars. A large Team Pendant logo was stenciled on each ramp and half pipe, as well as in the middle of the track, so any picture of Wulf would show the Pendant logo as well. *If Team Pendant spent as much time practicing here as they did thinking of ways to cheat,* Val thought, *they'd win more competitions.* Val settled to the ground near the ramps, behind a stack of tires used for cushioning and agility practice. He returned to his half-vampire shape and waited.

The charity exhibition was tomorrow, so the Extreme Monsters had been pretty sure Team Pendant would be practicing today. Val had agreed to sneak in and use his powers to protect Wulf from the Slime Brothers while Jinx and the others tried to find a spell that would cure him.

41

Val sat waiting for the reporters to show. It seemed to take forever. Then he heard approaching footsteps and ducked down. His half-vampire ears were amazingly sharp, so he could hear a whisper across a football field. He hoped that today that ability would help him keep Wulf in one piece.

Val peeked around the stacked tires. Damon Christopher and Wulf were entering the practice area. Wulf was waving his arms and talking wildly about saving the roller coaster. Wulf's signing hand was still a bit swollen. Damon was looking bored.

Val grinned.

With Damon watching, Wulf skated several ramps and rails, testing different grabs and grinds. Then he tried a brainless—he landed the backflip, but couldn't quite get around on 540 spin. The young werewolf stopped and frowned down at his skates.

"How do those blades compare with the ones Doc designed for you?" Damon asked in a fake-concerned voice.

Wulf looked confused. "Doc?" he asked.

"You know—Doc!" Damon snapped, obviously annoyed. "The skinny man with frizzy grey hair who designs the Extreme Monster's equipment! The one who used to work for me! The one who—"

"I've forgotten," Wulf said, looking even more confused. "Did *The* Extreme Monster have his own

designer that you fired?" He stared down at his skates some more. "It's a good thing because there's a bad rattle in these. The bearings aren't—"

"AREN'T WHAT? These skates are state-of-the-art design. Made with the finest materials the lowest bidder can supply, so as to maximize profit. You better listen to me! You use the equipment that is given to you without complaint or—" Damon shouted. The billionaire's face had grown crimson and his eyes were bulging.

Wulf looked at his new boss in alarm. "Whoa, dude! S' cool, s' cool! *The* Extreme Monster is so good, he can make even whack gear shine!"

Damon started to respond, but Wulf held up his hands and started for the track. "Look, dude, we don't have to talk about this Doc guy if it bothers you!" he said soothingly. "I have more important things to think about anyway! I need to find the perfect stunt that will save the Croney Island roller coaster from—

"Not that again!" Christopher practically howled. "Forget that stupid—"

Val snuck a quick look. He totally loathed Damon Christopher, so when he heard Damon's furious voice, he couldn't help grinning. Just talking to Wulf had Damon ready to pull out his carefully coiffed hair. For once, Val understood exactly how Damon felt.

Val's expression sobered. It was nice that Wulf was keeping quiet about Doc and the Extreme Monsters. Except he sounded real—like he honestly didn't remember anything about them. For the zillionth time, Val wondered what the Wild Magic had done to his werewolf friend.

Val heard more footsteps and voices and snuck another quick look. Reporters and cameramen were pouring onto the practice track. From one second to the next, the scowl disappeared from Damon Christopher's face, replaced by a bogus smile. "Come on, Wulf!" he said, placing a fatherly hand on Wulf's shoulder. "Let's say hello to your adoring public!"

Fifteen minutes later, the Slime Brothers stalked onto the practice track, dressed in yellow Team Pendant uniforms. They strolled nonchalantly toward the pack of reporters and photographers who were snapping pictures of Wulf catching air on the twelve-foot half pipe, but a swift scowl from Damon Christopher had them scurrying toward the racetrack across the yard. Very close to the stack of tires where Val was hiding.

Clem climbed on his Whisperboard, which came equipped with a miniature jet-powered engine. Cletus mounted his BMX bike. They took off together. It looked like they were racing innocently, but Val could hear them talking and knew better.

"Ain't right, that werewolf getting to be team star," Cletus said, heading his bike up a ramp, spinning the handlebars in a 360 cross-up, then throwing out both legs in a no-footer.

"Let that stupid werewolf top this!" Clem shouted, following his brother up the ramp and attempting a fakie 360 spin before landing on his whisperboard. Unfortunately, Clem missed the board and sprawled onto the track. "We've always been Team Pendant's stars!" Clem muttered, as he struggled to sit up.

"And we will be, again," Cletus agreed, holding out an oozing, sticky hand to help Clem stand. "All we have to do is get Wulf out of the way!"

Reporters shouted questions and cameramen filmed excitedly as Wulf clicked in on a caveman rail, then slid down in a blindside half-cab soul grind.

"What about the Extreme Monsters?" A reporter shouted as Wulf leapt from the rail. "Are they going to take your defection lying down?"

Wulf was beginning to get angry. "I am *The* Extreme Monster!" he said, for what seemed like the hundredth time. "Don't you get it?!"

He turned his back on the reporters and bladed angrily past Clem and Cletus who were standing on the track leading up to the first ramp. "Keep off the track, dudes," growled Wulf. "And keep out of my way!"

Clem looked at Cletus. Cletus looked at Clem. They smiled, their green faces revealing ugly yellow teeth, and put their hands behind their backs. Slime dripped down their fingers and plopped onto the ramp. Clem's ooze was slippery, and Cletus's ooze was sticky.

The Slime Brothers gave Wulf a venomous look. When Wulf struck either patch he was bound to spin out. With any luck he'd break something. Preferably his neck. "Whatever you say, Extreme Monster," Cletus said, leaping off the track. "Come on, bro'. Let's watch the man fall flat on his face." They went to stand with their backs to the stack of tires.

Val looked around. He was going to have to stop Wulf but he couldn't let Damon and his goons know he was there. He looked at the stack of tires. *Hmmmm!* he thought.

As Wulf began to skate down the track toward the ramp, Val picked up one of the tires and shoved it, hard, toward the track where the Slime Brothers had left their ooze. The tire bounced and rolled toward the track, drawing the attention of Damon, the reporters, and the Slime Brothers.

Seeing the tire roll across his path, Wulf leapt high over the obstacle, catching great air and totally missing the patches of slime. He landed in a hand plant on the edge of the ramp, flipped off, and skated toward the seven-foot ramp.

Reporters cheered. Cameras whirred and flashed. Everyone's eyes were on Wulf, so no one but Val saw the tire skid on the slimy ooze, stop short in the sticky ooze, and slam onto the ground. Val ooked at the mess and knew that it could have been Wulf. He knew there was a reason for coming here.

Damon rushed over. Seeing the thwarted looks on the faces of the Slime Brothers, he began to yell at them for throwing the tire and trying to injure their star skater.

Clem and Cletus backed up, protesting their innocence. They backed up so far that they bumped into the pillar of tires, which—with a little shove from Val—toppled, sending tires bouncing down all around them.

Val took this opportunity to turn himself back into mist. As Damon yelled, the cameramen took pictures, and, for once, Clem and Cletus were the focus of their attention. This was definitely not what either of them had had in mind.

Finally the reporters left. Val morphed into his half vampire form behind a wall, hoping Jinx had managed to work out an anti-hex.

Wulf was muttering again, trying to decide what stunt to do. It needed to be something spectacular. Something no one else had done before. He only had until tomorrow to come up with the goods.

PUZZLE 4

Directions:

Help Wulf avoid the Slime Brothers and impress the reporters! Only one path leads out of the maze and to the reporters. Help Wulf find the correct skate route.

Write the letter of the correct exit in the secret code box on page 93.

CHAPTER FIVE

Wulf's Awful Idea

Inside Val's garage, amid the fallen trophies, scattered equipment and overturned workbenches, Jinx sat on the concrete floor, holding a pen and yellow notepad, facing Steiner and Mumford.

"We've got to stop feeling guilty about what happened to Wulf and start using our heads to help him," she said.

Steiner and Mumford were nodding eagerly. *Who am I kidding? I probably feel guiltiest of all. I know how Wulf is...and how he sometimes has huge feelings he doesn't know how to handle. I shouldn't have let him get to me. I shouldn't have goaded him.* Jinx thought miserably.

"All right," Jinx said, trying to sound upbeat. "The first thing is the spell. I know Wulf started with the Forget Me spell, because that's what I was studying when he grabbed my opened book. It begins:

Ice cream, popcorn, lemon twist,
Forget me, pal, I don't exist.

Jinx wrote that down on her yellow notepad.

"That's bad enough. Luckily, it didn't work, because we can remember him." She looked up at the others. "Except, he kept waving my wand around and even a small dip of a wand can change the meaning of a phrase or turn it into its opposite."

"And don't forget, he kept throwing in other stuff," Mumford reminded her. "Something about a 'star,' I think! Or—yeah, it was 'superstar'!"

Jinx wrote down:

SUPERSTAR

"Then Wulf flipped to a different page and started reading the Invisibility Charm. Only he started somewhere in the middle." She grabbed her spell book and flipped through the pages. "That's eighth level, so I haven't really studied it yet, but I was reading ahead, so I recognized it. I think he started around here:

Air, clear water, ghostly pale,
May my magic never fail.

Jinx wrote it down carefully.

"Except, instead of 'never fail,' Wulf said 'bite my tail!'" said Steiner. "I remember because I thought it was funny."

Jinx groaned. Asking magic to 'bite your tail' was just plain stupid, and not the least bit funny. Magic was contrary and had a way of biting the hand that directed it, anyway, unless that hand was very careful.

She crossed out 'never fail,' and wrote down:

Bite my tail

"He read some other stuff," Mumford said.

"I know," Jinx agreed. She flipped though the spell book. "I think he read a bit of an Ego-Strengthening Charm, too! Only I don't know which one."

"He mentioned us somewhere in his spell. Except he said, Extreme Monster," Steiner said. "Just one."

"Yeah!" Mumford added. "And Team Pendant, too!"

On her yellow pad, Jinx wrote down:

Ego Charm

Then she wrote down:

Extreme Monster
Team Pendant

She looked at the others expectantly. "What else?"

Steiner and Mumford shrugged. "It was just gibberish," Steiner said. "Except for something about an 'amazing stunt' and the 'roller coaster.'"

"But it all rhymed!" Mumford reminded them. "I was really impressed. But that's all I remember!"

Jinx sighed and wrote down:

Amazing Stunt
Roller Coaster

"I don't remember any more, either," she said miserably. "I was too angry and upset to pay proper attention." She looked from Steiner to Mumford.

"I was watching Val," Steiner said.

Mumford nodded. "Me, too."

Jinx put her chin in her hands and stared at the others unhappily. "The truth is, we *have* to remember what Wulf said, not to mention what he did with my wand while he said it. If we can't, Wulf might be doomed!"

"C'mon, Jinx. You're the smartest one here. You'll figure out how to undo the spell," Steiner said.

"Besides, you're the only witch!" Mumford's eyes were big and pleading inside his bandages. "So you're the only one who can!"

Late that afternoon, Val was still watching, from his hiding place behind the tires in the Team Pendant practice yard. He was bored. After Val had toppled the tires—he grinned just thinking about it—the Slime Brothers had kept well away from Wulf. They were on the other side of the yard, watching Wulf do a double Ore-Ida, an alley-oop 720 that he landed on the half pipe, followed by a misty flip with a stalefish grab off a ramp.

Val put his head in his hands and closed his eyes. He'd seen Wulf practicing like a maniac plenty of times. How could he call Jinx's practice 'wimpy,' just because it involved a book? He smiled. Wulf wasn't always logical.

Val thought that perhaps it was time to head home. The benefit was tomorrow and Val needed to be practicing his stunts, too. Or at the very least helping Jinx figure out how to undo the hex. He figured that the Slime Brothers wouldn't go near Wulf now. Not after the scolding they got...Val jerked awake as his half-vampire ears picked up Clem's hoarse whisper across the yard.

"I can't believe that guy is still at it!" Clem muttered softly to his brother. "Wulf's totally hardcore!"

"Everything he does seems off the charts," Cletus admitted grudgingly. "But nothing he does makes him happy."

Clem was disgusted. "The only way that jerk's gonna be happy is if the stunt is so impossible nobody could do it and live!"

"Hey, bro'," Cletus whispered to Clem. "That's an idea. A darn fine idea!"

"Hunh?" grunted Clem. "Whaddaya mean?"

"Look. Wulf wants to do a spectacular stunt to save the roller coaster, right? And he's our teammate, and our new best pal, right?" Cletus said.

"Uh—nope?" Clem guessed.

Cletus punched him hard in the warty arm. "Pay attention! We pretend, see? We go over there and help the stupid werewolf think of a stunt so dangerous just trying it will put him in the hospital. Or worse!"

The Slime Brothers strolled over to the half pipe where Wulf was practicing. "Dude, you are the best blader we've ever seen," Cletus began. Wulf ignored him, soaring up the wall of the half pipe and into the air.

"Yeah, you must be like...a skating Einstein!" Clem added.

Wulf soared up the other wall, caught air, did a 180, and slid down again. He wasn't working out exactly. He was just keeping his body busy so his brain had time to think.

"And it's real noble of you to want to save that old roller coaster. I bet if the stunt you did was spectacular enough, you could save it single-handed. Without anybody else's help!" Cletus told him. "You just need a stunt that will showcase your incredible talent! After all, it's all about the roller coaster!"

That got Wulf's attention. He landed a cess slide and frowned at them. "A stunt?" Wulf said. "Something that involves the roller coaster?"

"That would be amazing!" Clem sighed. "But what?"

"I could blade beneath the pylons. Do my stunts there." Wulf said thoughtfully.

Cletus shook his head. "Too ordinary for a guy like you. The official stunt area is almost beneath the roller coaster anyway."

"Yeah, you're right!" Wulf muttered. "*The* Extreme Monster's stunt must be unique." He frowned.

Clem and Cletus waited.

"I've got it!" Wulf said. His red monster eyes began to glow excitedly. "What if I climb to the top of the coaster and blade down the rail!"

"Not bad!" Cletus said. "But is it wild enough?"

"While I'm doing it, I wear a League-standard Neutralizer Wristband to remove my monster powers!" Wulf suggested, looking excited.

"You're almost there!" cried Clem.

"Blindfolded!" shouted Wulf. "I'll blade the coaster without monster powers and blindfolded!"

Cletus and Clem high-fived each other. Slime oozed from their palms and splashed down around them. "Genius!" they chanted, with a horrible, warty double grin. The brothers clapped Wulf on the back with sticky fingers. "Why don't you go inside and tell the boss!"

As Wulf bladed off to the building, Clem and Cletus gave each other thumbs-up. Wulf was going to do more than go to the hospital. He was going to break his neck!

At least now that the Slime Brothers know Wulf is doomed, they'll lay off trying to hurt him, Val thought as he turned to mist and floated over the wall. That was the only good thing that had come out of this day. He hoped Jinx had found a way to reverse that awful spell. As he hovered in midair, Val turned back into a half-vampire boy. He picked up his board where he had hidden it and skated for home. *It wouldn't hurt if Jinx's cure included some way to make Wulf forget this insane stunt, either,* Val thought.

PUZZLE 5

Directions:

Match the questions with the answers. When you are done, there will be one answer left over.

Questions:

1. What line did Wulf say in the spell that Steiner thought was funny? ___

2. Who felt the guiltiest of all about the spell accidently cast on Wulf? ___

3. Name the monsters who pretend to be Wulf's friends. ___

4. What is the last thing Wulf decides to do for his stunt? ___

Answers:

a. wear a blindfold
b. bite my tail
c. Jinx
d. Neutralizer Wristband
e. Clem and Cletus

Write the letter of the unused answer in the secret code box on page 93.

CHAPTER SIX

Let the Games Begin!

Jinx sat cross-legged on the floor of Val's garage, trying to figure out what Wulf had done. Hoping that peace and quiet might help her think, she had sent Steiner and Mumford to the Extreme Sports Park to practice their stunts for the benefit.

Which was tomorrow.

Jinx rested her chin on her hand and studied the list she had written carefully on the yellow pad. It wasn't long. It wasn't encouraging, either. And it did little to explain why Wulf would suddenly leave the Extreme Monsters and join their rivals. Or did it?

The list said:

> Ice cream, popcorn, lemon twist,
> Forget me, pal, I don't exist
> Air, clear water, ghostly pale,
> May my magic, BITE MY TAIL

SUPERSTAR
EGO CHARM
EXTREME MONSTER
TEAM PENDANT
AMAZING STUNT
ROLLER COASTER

Making sure her wand was lying safely beside her, Jinx whispered:

Ice-cream, popcorn, lemon twist
Forget me, pal, I don't exist.

The spell must have disturbed Wulf's memory, she thought.

Jinx drew a line down the center of the paper, and on the other side wrote:

Memory

Okay, she thought. What's next? Jinx whispered:

Air, clear water, ghostly pale,
May my magic...

Bite my tail, she thought, and shuddered. She couldn't even make herself whisper the phrase out loud. Wulf didn't know it, of course, but he had been asking

60

for trouble.

It was part of an Invisibility Charm. She wrote

Invisibility

under MEMORY on her new list.

Except nobody's invisible, she thought. Not Wulf. Not us. So where did the invisibility go?

She sighed and went on to the next line.

Superstar

The spell did get him on TV, she thought. But joining Team Pendant was more like joining the Ghost Club of Extreme Sports than being a superstar. He would go in with fanfare like most of the new Pendant members, but when it came down to it, Damon Christopher was the only star of Team Pendant.

She looked at her list. Nothing else there should do much harm. She hoped. Jinx wished she knew what else Wulf had said. "I'll just have to work with what I know!" she muttered. "Memory, for instance. Maybe Wulf is acting weird because his memory has been scrambled."

She thought back to the press conference when he'd looked right through her and knew she'd found at least part of the answer. *I'll create a spell to restore his memory,* she thought. *But I'll have to be careful. I don't know what other kinds of magic Wulf invoked. I wouldn't want to do more harm than good.* Again Jinx thought of the phrase 'bite my tail' and shuddered.

Looking around for more clues, she studied the destruction caused by Wulf's misguided use of magic. The overturned workbenches. The tools scattered around the garage. The equipment and trophies smashed on the floor. Whatever Wulf had done, the spell was powerful. Even Wild Magic didn't usually explode like that.

Jinx could hear Steiner and Mumford returning from practice. She stood up. Maybe the clutter was making it hard to think. She'd go outside, say hi to her teammates, and then head next door to work on the counter-spell in her room.

As Jinx stepped out the side door, she saw Val skate up the driveway. At the same time, Steiner and Mumford were rolling up the sidewalk, with Mumford skitching as usual. They spotted Val and waved excitedly.

"Val!" Mumford shouted. "How's Wulf? Is he okay?"

"For now," said Val, sounding discouraged.

Jinx could tell from Val's voice that something was wrong.

But Mumford didn't notice. He ordered his bandage to let go of the bike and ran toward Jinx. "Did you figure out how to undo the spell?"

"Not completely," Jinx said. "But I know how to begin. I need to restore Wulf's memory."

62

Val frowned. "You might be right. I honestly think he doesn't remember we exist."

"I'll create a spell to fix that. We'll try it on him and see what happens. Then we'll see what else needs tweaking."

Val frowned. "How long will that take?"

"Two or three days to create the spell," Jinx said. "We don't know exactly what we're dealing with so I have to be really careful."

Val sighed. "That's not soon enough. We have a problem. Come inside, everybody. It's got to be all over Damon's Extreme Sports Channel by now."

Jinx settled in with Val, Steiner, and Mumford on the sofa in Val's den. Val clicked the remote and the Team Pendant logo flashed on the screen. Then Damon Christopher appeared.

Jinx scowled. Damon looked like a well-groomed, expensively dressed snake.

"Tomorrow, at the Croney Island benefit," Damon announced, "Team Pendant's newest and greatest superstar, Wulf, will perform a stunt never attempted by another blader, anywhere. Wulf will blade down the tracks of the roller coaster—blindfolded."

"He'll WHAT?" roared Steiner.

Val shrugged. "You heard the man."

"But that roller coaster is in terrible shape," Jinx

63

said. "The tracks and support structures are falling apart. Not to mention that the peaks are way off the ground. And he wants to do it *blindfolded?!*"

Mumford shook his head in denial. "No way! That can't be right! It's way too dangerous to do tricks up there—even if you aren't blindfolded."

"Yeah, man," Steiner said, laying a giant hand on Mumford's shoulder. "That's not brave. That's stupid."

"Stupid? Definitely," said Jinx. "But it makes a horrible kind of sense. Remember, Wulf mentioned the stunt and the roller coaster in his spell. I think it's all tied together. I wish we knew exactly what he had said."

Jinx stood up. "I'm going home to work on a counter-spell," she said. "Maybe if I stay up all night, I can get the memory-restoring part finished by tomorrow."

"Good," said Val. "Because, from now until Wulf is cured, our number one priority is keeping him alive."

Val, Steiner, and Mumford trooped into the garage.

Steiner slumped down on the floor and started to disassemble and clean the bearings in the rear sprocket of his bike. Mumford watched morosely, rousing himself from time to time to lasso a tool from among the chaos and hand it to Steiner.

But Val was too restless to sit. He began to talk, telling his friends how the Slime Brothers had tried to

make Wulf wipe out on the ramp, then goaded him into inventing that ridiculous stunt. As Val talked, he began systematically to turn workbenches upright and hang equipment back on hooks, sweeping the broken parts into a corner.

Finally the garage was almost back to normal. Val righted one last workbench. "Hey, look what I found," he said, holding up Mumford's video camera.

"I don't want it," said Mumford. "That's what started Wulf acting so crazy—showing off for the camera."

"It's not the camera's fault," said Val, holding his eye to the lens and pushing the ON button. Nothing happened. "Hey, didn't you have a brand-new battery in this thing?"

"Maybe," said Mumford uncertainly. "I don't think I'm very good with cameras."

"No problem," said Val, grabbing a cord and plugging the camera into an outlet. "We'll recharge it and see what you have. Maybe it's better than you think."

"If it's wiggly, fuzzy pictures of Wulf acting like a jerk," Mumford muttered, "I don't want to watch."

But, of course, he did.

Val plugged the recharged camera into the computer in his bedroom. Val, Steiner, and Mumford watched Wulf skating around and showing off on the screen. The camera had captured the beginning of Wulf's argument with Jinx and showed Val stepping—well, flying—in to try and calm things down.

"It's not that bad, Mumford," Val said encouragingly. "Maybe all you need to do is practice."

"And read the lame instruction book," Steiner said with a grin.

On the computer screen the argument between Jinx and Wulf grew more heated. Suddenly the computer image spun around the garage and turned sideways.

"What happened?" Steiner asked.

"Val told me to put the camera away," said Mumford miserably. "I was making Wulf show off too much. So I tossed it on the workbench."

"It wasn't you," said Val. On the computer screen,

the scene was continuing, only sideways. The friends leaned sideways and watched as Val and Steiner tried to calm Wulf down. And Wulf grabbed Jinx's book...and began his spell. They watched open-mouthed as Wulf read some words and made up others while he skated backwards in a circle.

"The camera was still on," Mumford murmured. "I guess I didn't turn it off when I put it down."

"And the lens was facing us. It recorded everything," Val agreed.

"Jinx!" Val cried suddenly, as he launched himself out the bedroom window, headed for her house. "Jinx! We know what Wulf said! Come and see!"

PUZZLE 6

Directions:

Figure out which workbench the video camera is under. Use the clues to mark off a workbench until only one is left.

a. It isn't under the smallest workbench.
b. It isn't under the workbench in the center.
c. It isn't under the workbench with three drawers.
d. It isn't under the tallest workbench.

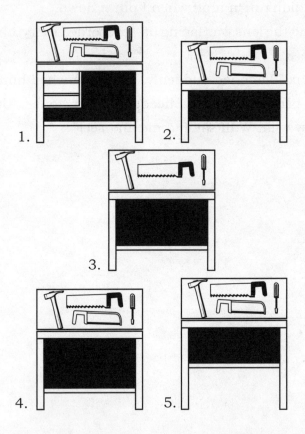

Write the number of the correct workbench in the secret code box provided on page 93.

CHAPTER SEVEN
What Wulf Said and What Jinx Does

It was late. But Jinx, Val, Mumford, and Steiner were monsters. Their parents, who were mostly monsters, too, thought it only natural that their children stay up past midnight.

So, as the three guys waited, Jinx carefully wrote down the final words to Wulf's spell. She underlined the parts Wulf made up himself.

Then she read the spell out to the others:

> *Ice cream, popcorn, lemon twist,*
> *Forget me, pal, I don't exist!*
>
> *Never was and never been,*
> *Gonna take it for a spin!*

This had been accompanied by a 360 spin high into the air and wild waving of the wand. Jinx could only hope she would be able to undo that one entirely.

Air, clear water, ghostly pale,
May this magic bite my tail.

"Wulf has definitely wiped us from his memory," Jinx said. "And from his sight as well!"

"What does that mean?" Mumford asked timidly.

Jinx smiled sadly. "It means he can no longer see any Extreme Monster but himself."

"That's why he's been acting like he never heard of us! Why he looks right through us! The magic makes us not exist in wulf's eyes." Steiner exclaimed.

Jinx read:

Chocolate, peanut, candy bar,
Superego, Superstar!

Mirror, mirror on the wall,
Extreme Monster standing tall!

"See? Wulf just sees himself. As far as Wulf remembers, we don't exist. That's why he's *The* Extreme Monster! There's more:"

Extreme Monster, super cool,
Dumb Team Pendant pays the fool!

"That's the part that made Wulf go work for Team Pendant," Jinx told the others. "He probably meant to say 'plays' instead of 'pays.' Which shows how careful you have to be when you say spells."

Amazing stunt with hocus-pocus,
High to high and low to low-cus,

Roller coaster going down,
Rumble, tumble! Look out, clown!

Jinx frowned. The last line had her worried. She hoped the magic wasn't planning to knock down the roller coaster when everyone was beneath it.

Val frowned grumpily. "Did the spell wipe out whatever good sense Wulf once had, too?"

Steiner raised his eyebrows. "Wulf once had good sense?"

At that, even Jinx smiled a little.

The words to Wulf's spell, along with Wulf's accompanying gestures, gave Jinx the hints she needed to create an effective counter-spell fairly quickly. She worked all night, and by 10:00 the next morning, the counter-spell was almost done. Jinx just had to *poof*-read the spell for mistakes and make sure she had memorized it perfectly. She didn't want Wulf to end up in even worse trouble.

"You three go on to the park," Jinx called from her bedroom window when she saw them arriving next door. "I'll finish up the counter-spell and take my broom. I'll get there as fast as I can. Ask the officials to save Wulf's stunt for the grand finale. And whatever happens, keep him alive!"

As the monsters arrived at Croney Island, they heard the roar of voices. They knew the press would be there along with the other extreme sports stars. They also expected to see a few hundred wealthy philanthropists and hardcore spectators. What they hadn't expected were thousands of fans shouting for Wulf to come out and do his death-defying stunt.

They found Doc with his Laboratory Utility Vehicle (Doc called it his "L.U.V.") and their equipment. Val updated Doc on the Wulf situation and told him Jinx would be there later but that she was opting out of the demonstrations. Doc understood. She had more important things on her mind right now.

Damon Christopher's Team Pendant arrived in the stretch Hummer, which stopped beside the spectacular Team Pendant trailer. Pendant posters advertised gear, T-shirts and other products everywhere a photo might conceivably be taken.

Dressed in a bright yellow Team Pendant uniform, Wulf was greeted with a tumultuous roar of excitement. He waved his still-swollen hand to the crowd. Damon Christopher, looking especially dapper and well groomed, climbed out behind him.

"Doc and the Extreme Monsters are here somewhere," Damon murmured to Wulf. "Don't let their presence rattle you!"

Wulf rolled his eyes. There it was again—that strange reference to some group he'd never heard of. And why were they using his name?

"Dude, how many times do I have to say it? I'm The one-and-only Extreme Monster!" Wulf said calmly. "The world will realize that after I've done my stunt!" He stared affectionately up at the rickety old roller coaster. It seemed to be leaning a bit to one side. Probably an optical illusion, he thought. Everything will be fine.

Wulf turned to Damon. "Dude, I can't tell you how much I'm looking forward to riding those rails again!"

Damon put a fatherly hand on Wulf's shoulder. "Excellent!" he said. "And this time the world will see you do it—wearing the Team Pendant colors!"

"The stunt Wulf's about to do is crazy, but he doesn't look worried," said Mumford. "What's wrong with him?"

"I'm not sure, Mum-Man," said Steiner. "But I think the magic is making him think it's okay."

"Remind me never to go near that spell book," Val said with a shudder.

"Hey, look!" said Mumford. "His hand is still swollen. At least Jinx kept him from signing the contract!"

The Extreme Monsters watched Damon shepherd

Wulf into the Team Pendant trailer, as the rest of Damon's team climbed from the Hummer and posed for photos in front of the merchandise.

"The Slime Brothers are looking very happy with themselves," Steiner muttered.

"They should be," Val agreed. "For once, their trick is working!"

"Omigosh!" Mumford gasped, "They have Team Pendant logos stenciled on their teeth!"

"Yuck! At least Wulf hasn't gone that far," Val said. "Let's see if we can find T. Rexford Snattly and get him to stop Wulf. Or at least put him last on the program."

T. Rexford Snattly—a little round man who liked to be called T. Rex—was the Extreme Team Sports League president and the emcee of today's special demonstration. The Extreme Monsters found him talking chummily to Damon Christopher.

"Doesn't ol' T. Rex ever learn?" Mumford said.

"I don't think he's very smart," Steiner agreed.

"Come on!" said Val. "Let's get this over with. The stunt demos are supposed to start soon!"

"Mr. Snattly?" Val said politely, approaching the two adults. Snattly and Damon looked down at Val and the others. Damon's grin became particularly predatory.

Val ignored him. "Sir, we wondered if Wulf's stunt could be saved, sort of, for the grand finale?"

"Because your stunts will seem pathetically

ordinary next to Wulf's spectacular demonstration?" Damon asked snidely.

"No!" Val said indignantly. "It's just that—"

T. Rex broke in. "Now, Damon, don't bait the boy! Sorry, my boy. I've already agreed to let Wulf go first. After all, it's his proposed stunt that has brought out the crowd and brought in the donations."

The three teammates trudged toward Doc's van.

"How can T. Rex let something like that go through?" Val asked.

"Wulf put the stunt in his magic spell," Steiner reminded him. "That's probably influencing T. Rex as much as Damon is."

"I wish Jinx would get here," Mumford muttered, looking around worriedly.

"She said she'd hurry," Val said. "We'll have to trust her to do just that."

Jinx was saying the spell to herself while practicing hand movements. It was the most complex spell she had ever written and she wanted to get every word and gesture right. Wulf's life might depend on it. Bela the bat perched in his favorite spot on the tip of her hat. He had heard the spell so many times he could practically squeak it himself. As Jinx mounted her broom and soared out her window toward the park, she was still muttering the words under her breath.

*****

The Croney Island roller coaster loomed drunkenly over the demo area.

Temporary stands filled with excited spectators lined the dirt track along its base. The track held ramps of varying heights, and in the center, almost beneath the roller coaster, were half pipes and verts

But right now, every eye in the audience was fixed on Wulf as he climbed the maintenance ladder to the top peak of the roller coaster, over 100 feet off the ground. His skates were tied together and slung over his shoulder. Val, Mumford, and Steiner, watching from below, could hear the wooden posts and girders creak.

At the highest point of the roller coaster, Wulf sat and laced on his skates. He stood on his blades and, dramatically, snapped on the Neutralizer Wristband, which would prevent him from using his monster powers while doing the stunt.

"Whoa, look at that!" Steiner said. "Look at his hand! It suddenly went down to normal size."

"The Neutralizer must have removed the last trace of Jinx's hand hex!" Val said.

"Look how mad Damon is," said Mumford, nudging the others. "He knows now for sure that Wulf was enchanted to keep him from signing. I think he's looking around for Jinx."

"So am I," Val muttered. But Jinx was nowhere in sight.

"Hey, wait a minute," said Mumford. "If the

Neutralizer stopped Jinx's spell, why didn't it stop the spell that caused all this?"

Val shook his head. "I'm not sure, but my guess would be that the Wild Magic spell is too much for the Neutralizer Wristband. It should—"

"Look up!" said Steiner interrupting Val. "Wulf's about to take the plunge!"

High above, Wulf pulled a Team Pendant scarf from

his pocket and waved it around theatrically. Then he tied it around his eyes. Mumford's bandaged hands covered his face. "I can't watch!" he said.

Wulf launched himself down the left rail, going like lightning, beginning with a backside grind, spinning to a blindside half cab soul grind on the right rail.

The problem came when he began his Berani—a front flip with a 180 spin back toward the left rail.

Even blindfolded, Wulf executed the move perfectly. But as he landed, the rotten wooden strut that held the rail directly beneath him shattered and the rusty rail bent. The roller coaster lurched and swayed. Blindfolded and without his powers, Wulf tumbled through the tracks and plummeted toward the ground.

PUZZLE 7

Directions:

Below are lines that were said in the previous chapter. Write the name of the character who said the line on the space provided. Once you've done that, you'll see that some letters are in boxes. Unscramble those letters to spell out a number.

_ ☐ _ ☐ "It means he can no longer see any Extreme Monster but himself."

☐. _ ☐ _ "Now, Damon, don't bait the boy!"

_ _ _ _ ☐ "Don't let their presence rattle you!"

_ _ _ _ "Dude, how many times do I have to say it?"

☐_ _ _ _ ☐ _ "Wulf's about to take the plunge!"

Write the unscrambled number in the secret code box provided on page 93.

CHAPTER EIGHT

The Counter-Spell

"Wulf!" yelled Val. He hurled himself into the air and soared toward his flailing friend. Fast as he was, he knew he would be too late.

Suddenly a voice rang out high above him:

> *Broken strut and twisted rail,*
> *Let a splinter grab your tail!*

Wulf's tail fur snagged on a splintered strut.

"Ouch!" screamed Wulf, grabbing his wounded tail. "What happened?" Wulf yanked the blindfold from his eyes and saw he was dangling by his tail, five stories above the ground. He flailed his arms, trying to grab hold of the strut. His tail began to slip.

"Wulf! Don't!" Val yelled. "Hold still!"

But, though Val was flying toward him and Jinx was circling overhead on her broom, Wulf couldn't see or hear either one of them. He reached out again, trying to grab a cross-beam, and slipped some more.

Once again the rickety structure surrounding him swayed alarmingly.

Bela the bat flew at Val, squeaking, "Crack! Crack in the wood!" and fluttered off toward a cross-brace.

Now Val could see one of the main cross-girders beginning to give way. "You help Wulf!" Val called up to Jinx. "We'll try to hold the roller coaster together!" Val swooped down to grab Mumford, but Mumford was already climbing toward the cracked cross-brace.

"I see it, Val," he called out, as he climbed like a spider, extending a bandage into the air, grabbing the next beam, and hauling himself up. "I'll take care of it."

Val wasn't surprised. Mumford's specialty was speed climbing. He was completely fearless about heights. Just because Mumford was little didn't mean he wasn't smart and fast.

"Thanks, Mum-Man," Val called to the young mummy. But as he turned to fly back toward Wulf, the structure shook and lurched again. Val looked around in alarm, sure the entire section was about to crumble. If it did, the whole fragile roller coaster would come tumbling down like a house of cards. *Just like in Wulf's spell!* Val groaned.

Once again, the structure settled. Val looked down and saw Steiner at the bottom of the roller coaster, his huge hands braced against the major load-bearing beam, shoving with all his monster strength.

Val looked up. Mumford had reached his cross-brace and was wrapping one of his bandages quickly and carefully around the cracking area. So far, the repair was holding.

Val flew toward Jinx. "I like the way you made the magic bite Wulf's tail to save him," he said with a momentary grin. "So, what's the hold-up?"

Jinx bit her lip. "Wulf's wearing his Neutralizer Wristband. I'm afraid my counter-spell will just bounce off him! Even if it doesn't, the shock of the magic hitting him might send him plummeting to the ground."

"I'll grab the wristband," Val said. "Then you zap him. And don't worry, I'll catch him if he falls!"

As Val flew toward the dangling Wulf, he studied his friend carefully. He knew what he had to do.

Wulf felt a tug on his arm as the Neutralizer Wristband seemed to slide magically from his wrist.

He watched it float for a second in midair, then fall five long stories to the ground below.

"Whoa, dude," Wulf muttered to himself. "That could have been *The* Extreme Monster!"

"All right," Val shouted up to Jinx. "Let Wulf have it—NOW!"

Val hovered beneath the dangling Wulf as Jinx began to wave her wand and chant her well rehearsed spell:

Chocolate, berry, licorice chew,

You know us and we know you!

Mended eyes no longer mar
Your sight. You see us as we are.

We're your pals and you're our friend!
Let your scrambled memory mend.

Jinx waved her wand in a squiggly circle, trying to move it exactly opposite to Wulf's earlier, chaotic gesture. She held her breath and waited.

Wulf's eyes suddenly went blank and his body jerked hard in shock. For a second, he hung there. Then his tail pulled loose, and he fell.

Val, flying below, grabbed Wulf around his chest and held on tight.

"Hunh?" Wulf asked. "Who? What? Val—what are you doing grabbing *The* Extreme Monster?"

"It half worked," Val called to Jinx. "But he still thinks—"

"I heard," Jinx yelled. "There's more." Waving her wand again, she chanted:

Mirror, Mirror on the wall,
All together, standing tall!

Extreme Monster! Super-friend!
Let your star-fixation end!"

Again she waited.

Wulf looked around. He blinked. Then he looked over his shoulder at Val and grinned. "Dude!" he said. "What're you and me doing all the way up here?"

Perched on her broom, Jinx was beaming. Wulf was himself again. For better or worse. Which was just how they liked him.

"Hey, Jinx! A little help down here?" Steiner shouted.

"Oh!" said Jinx. "Sorry!"

She swooped downward, chanting:

Roller coaster hold like glue,
Steady, solid, all day through!

She stared at the roller coaster. Yes, she could see it—the ripple of magic shoring up the teetering structure.

"Okay, Steiner," she called out. "It's safe to let go now! I've got it."

Slowly, Steiner pulled his hands away. The rickety construction held. "Come on down, Mumford," Steiner called. And Mumford obediently began to climb toward the ground.

Val, Wulf, and Jinx landed at the same time.

"Dudette, thanks," Wulf said. "But if you could fix this crusty, old roller coaster any time you wanted, why didn't you?"

"Because..." said Jinx faintly. Val saw that Jinx's green-tinged skin had become chalk white. "Because..." she began again. Jinx collapsed from her broom in a dead faint.

Steiner caught her before she hit the ground. "Because, you doofus," Val said to Wulf, "doing magic properly takes a lot out of a person. It's her personal energy that's holding up that roller coaster. And if they don't get some scaffolding soon, it's going to crash down around us!"

"Oh!" said Wulf.

Suddenly, they heard a deafening roar. The audience in the temporary stands was going wild, cheering and shouting the names of the Extreme Monsters.

"Some stunt!" Damon Christopher sneered nastily as he walked up to Wulf, who was standing with his friends, trying to revive Jinx. "You almost collapsed the whole structure! Plus you had to be rescued by your ridiculous little ex-teammates!"

"Ex-teammates?" Wulf said, looking confused.

"Long story," Val murmured. "You zapped yourself with magic. You couldn't see or hear us. You joined Team Pendant."

"No way!" Wulf said. "I wouldn't!"

"Have you seen what you're wearing?" Mumford asked.

Wulf looked down at his Team Pendant uniform. "Dude! I HATE puke yellow!" he screamed, tearing at the jersey to get out of it. "Get it off me! Oh man, I didn't sign a contract, did I? Tell me I didn't."

"You didn't," Val told him. "Thanks to Jinx."

Wulf handed the torn jersey back to Damon. "Here," he said. "Take it. I don't want it. I'm off your team! Forever!"

Damon snatched the torn jersey and stalked away angrily. Behind his back, Clem and Cletus high-fived each other with slimy hands and lurched happily toward the Team Pendant trailer.

The rest of the show was called off because of the condition of the roller coaster. Braces were brought in to shore up the crumbling structure. The stands were being cleared and the audience herded toward the exit. Reporters surrounded the Extreme Monsters.

"Did you know your proposal to blade the roller coaster blindfolded and without monster powers drew record donations for its restoration?" one reporter asked.

"I said I'd do what? What am I, a moron?" Wulf whispered in horror.

Jinx looked at Val and both gave a little snicker.

"Was your defection to Team Pendant part of a publicity stunt to draw attention to the benefit?" asked a blue-skinned reporter from *The Witchly Whisper.*

"Are you happy that people really enjoyed the show, even if it featured more super-heroics than extreme sports, and you had to be rescued?" a human asked with a sneer.

They looked to Wulf for comment. But Wulf just looked confused.

"Like I said," Val murmured. "Long story. Probably the less said right now, the better."

"Whatever you say," Wulf agreed, with uncharacteristic humility. "No comment," he told the reporters.

"Come on, dudes," Wulf told his friends, "Let's find Doc. You can fill me in at Mr. Cool's!"

*****

"...And that's how it all happened." Val finished the tale of their recent exploits. He took a final sip of his sparkling beet juice as the others demolished their ice cream.

"Sorry, Jinx," Wulf said. "I acted like a total jerk."

"You did!" said Mumford. "You had us worried to death!"

"Hush!" Jinx told Mumford. "I acted like a jerk, too, Wulf. I shouldn't have gotten so mad. It just escalated the problem."

"No," Wulf said. "I started it. It was definitely me acting like I was so great. If it hadn't been for you dudes' teamwork, I'd be fried bacon!"

"Um, Jinx," Val whispered. "You didn't...do something to Wulf? He's being so...so humble."

"I know," Jinx said, frowning at Wulf worriedly. "I think it's just a reaction...like having a fever after you get a shot. It should wear off."

"Excellent," Val said with a grin. "In that case, let's enjoy it while we can! You know, Wulf," he continued. "since its all your fault, I think the next round of snacks should be on you!"

"Yeah, okay," Wulf agreed. "That sounds fair."

Jinx looked at Val. Val looked at Jinx. They looked at Steiner, Mumford, and Doc, whose mouths were hanging open.

"Hey! Wait a minute!" said Wulf, sounding indignant, and much more like his old self. "What am I saying? Who says it was my fault?"

"Whew," said Val.

"That didn't last long," said Jinx.

And Val, Jinx, Mumford, Steiner, and Doc burst out laughing. A second later, Wulf was laughing with them, the loudest of all.

PUZZLE 8

Directions:

All the Extreme Monsters names are hidden in the word hunt below. (Be careful! The words may read from right to left or from down to up.) Don't forget that the team has members that don't participate in the actual events! When you have found all the words, start at the upper left and copy the letters that have not been used into the spaces for the "secret message."

E	R	J	I	G	B	H	C
T	E	C	I	E	A	B	O
O	N	W	L	N	V	H	D
X	I	A	P	A	X	G	S
C	E	F	L	U	W	R	B
J	T	V	L	A	U	X	N
E	S	I	M	L	T	Z	Z
D	R	O	F	M	U	M	B

BELA	DOC	JINX	MUMFORD
STEINER	VAL	WULF	

SECRET MESSAGE: __ __ __ __ __

Write the number in the secret code box provided on page 93.

90

SECRET CODE

Directions:

Write your answers in the space under the puzzle number.

CODE KEY

Puzzle No.	1	2	3	4	5	6	7	8
Answer								

And now visit

www.extrememonsters.com
and type in the secret code from the
code key above.

You'll unlock extra games and features.

Plus, you'll learn more about the Extreme
Monsters and their thrilling world!

If you need help with any of the puzzles, an
answer key can be found on the website too!

GLOSSARY

360   *(skating, skateboarding, BMX)* Spinning completely around so you end up facing the same direction you started facing.

540   (skating, skateboarding, BMX) Spinning around one complete revolution plus another half revolution.

360 cross up   *(skating)* A spin with one foot behind the other (legs crossed)

Back flip   *(skating, skateboarding, BMX)* Doing a backward somersault in the air.

Berani   *(skating)* A front flip with a 180 in it.

Blindside   *(skating, skateboarding, BMX)* Any trick done with your back to the obstacle.

Brainless   *(skating, skateboarding, BMX)* A backflip with a 540 spin done on a ramp.

Cess slide   *(skating)* Sliding sideways on both skates to stop.

Double Ore-Ida   *(skating, skateboarding, BMX)* Vert trick in which you turn one way while rotating two complete revolutions.

Fakie   *(skating, skateboarding)* Any move or trick done backwards.

Freewheel   *(BMX)* The device attached to the back hub that the chain goes around and catches so that you can pedal forward and move or not pedal while the wheel still spins.

Frontside   *(skateboarding)* Any trick done while facing an obstacle.

Grab   *(skating, skateboarding)* To reach down and grab your skate or board.

Grind   *(skating, skateboarding, BMX)* Sliding along an edge using your trucks, pegs, or the side of your skates.

Half Cab	*(skating)* Going from skating backwards to skating forwards
Half Pipe	*(skating, skateboarding, BMX)* A type of ramp that looks much like a "U."
High caveman rail	*(skateboarding)* Start holding the board in your hands, run, and jump with your board onto a high rail and slide or grind.
Kickflip	*(skateboard)* In a kickflip, the skater kicks the board with the ball of his or her front foot, the skateboard flips and spins over at least once, and the skateboarder lands on the board comfortably, wheels down, and rides away.
Misty flip	*(skating, skateboarding)* A front flip that is performed sideways.
No-footer	*(BMX)* To kick your feet backward off the pedals.
Rail	*(skating, skateboarding, BMX)* Metal bar that you grind on.
Skitching	*(skateboard, skating)* Being towed by a rope (or bandage) from a bicycle.
Soul grind	*(skating)* A type of grind in which the front foot is perpendicular like a normal frontside, but the back foot is parallel to the rail.
Stalefish Grab	*(skating, skateboarding)* To reach behind you and grab the outside of the opposite skate or back edge of your board.
Tailslide	*(skateboard)* Sliding on the tail of the board.
Vert	*(skating, skateboarding, BMX)* Term used to describe any half pipe that goes vertical at the top. It is usually around 8-12 feet high.